D0842284

Which Way Should I Go?

Which Way Should I go?

SYLVIA OLSEN
WITH RON MARTIN

Illustrated by
KASIA CHARKO

sononis
PRESS
WINLAW, BRITISH COLUMBIA

Library and Archives Canada Cataloguing in Publication

Olsen, Sylvia, 1955-
Which way should I go? / Sylvia Olsen with Ron Martin ; illustrated by Kasia Charko.

ISBN 978-1-55039-161-9

I. Nootka Indians—Juvenile fiction. 2. Nootka Indians—Social life and customs—Juvenile fiction. 3. Grief—Juvenile fiction. I. Martin, Ron, 1957- II. Charko, Kasia, 1949- III. Title.

PS8579.L728W46 2007 jC813'.6 C2007-905048-4

Sono Nis Press most gratefully acknowledges support for our publishing program provided by the Government of Canada through the Book Publishing Industry Development Program (BPIDP) and the Canada Council for the Arts, and by the Province of British Columbia through the British Columbia Arts Council and the Book Publishing Tax Credit, Ministry of Provincial Revenue.

Edited by Laura Peetoom
Copy edited by Dawn Loewen
Cover and interior design by Jim Brennan

Published by
SONO NIS PRESS
Box 160
Winlaw, BC V0G 2J0
1-800-370-5228
1-250-226-0077

Distributed in the U.S. by
Orca Book Publishers
Box 468
Custer, WA 98240-0468
1-800-210-5277

books@sononis.com
www.sononis.com

Printed and bound in Canada by Friesens Printing

Ron Martin dedicates this book to his daughter Courtney, his many nephews and nieces, their children and their children's children

FREE
99¢
COFFEE

Joey was a happy boy. Almost every day he was in a good mood.

When Simon, his best friend, asked Joey why he was always smiling, Joey said, "Because I'm happy!"

When Mrs. Walker, his teacher, asked him why he so seldom got discouraged with his school work when it was difficult, Joey said, "Because I like to look at the bright side of things."

When Mr. Smith, the man at the store, asked him why he carried groceries so enthusiastically, Joey said, "Because I like being helpful."

But there was something Joey didn't tell Simon, Mrs. Walker, and Mr. Smith. There was a reason Joey was happy. There was a reason he liked to be helpful and look on the bright side of things. It was the same reason he liked to visit his grandma.

Joey's grandma was his favourite person in the whole world. When he visited her house she made him applesauce. She would ask him, "Would you like cinnamon with your applesauce? Would you like ice cream with your applesauce?"

Sometimes Joey chose applesauce with cinnamon and sometimes he chose applesauce with ice cream. Sometimes he even chose to put raisins in his applesauce. It was fun to choose.

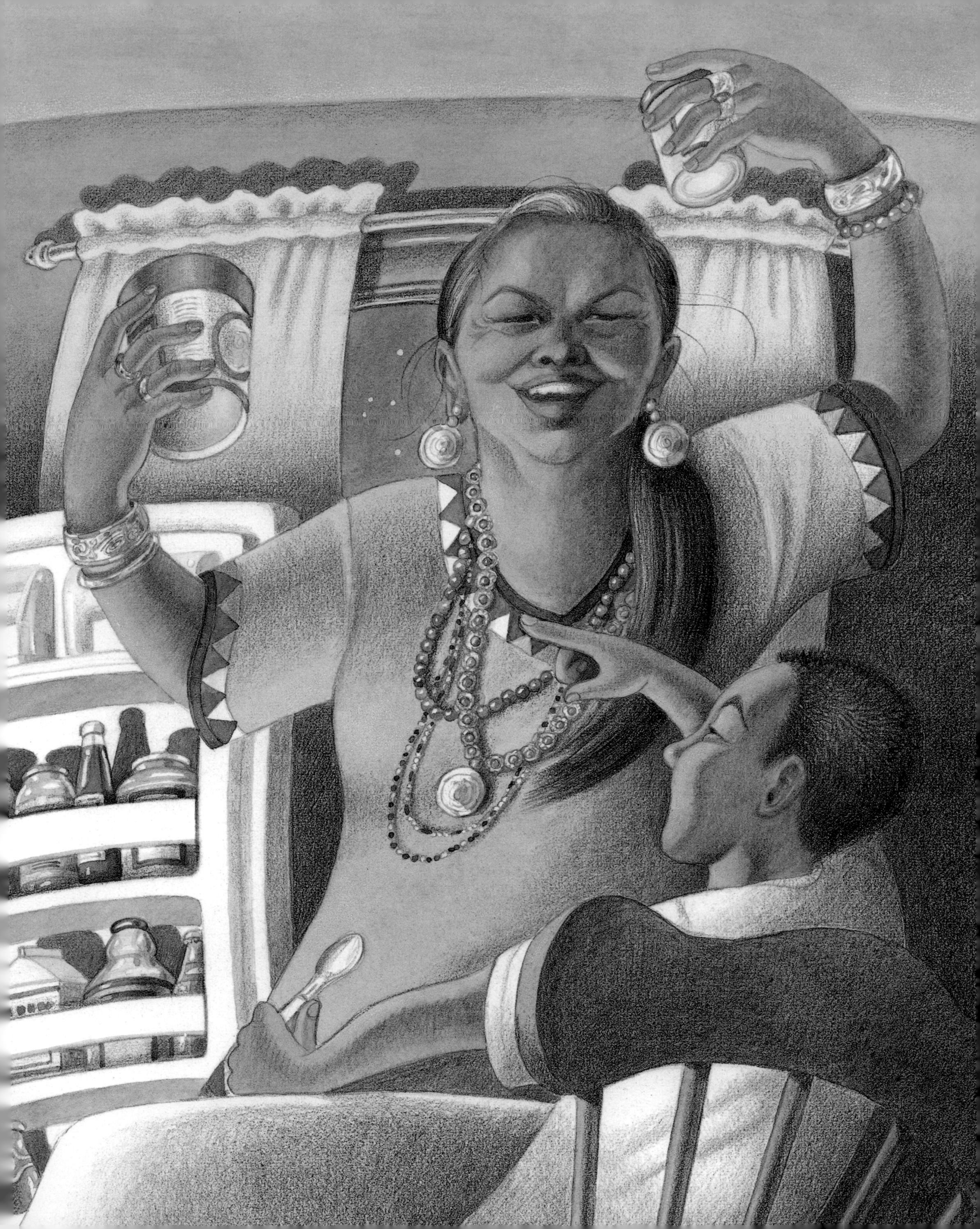

After Joey ate his applesauce, Grandma would sing a song with him.

Aah yee ha, aah yee ha
Waa yee seekee ahh kuu
Waa yee seekee ahh kuu

Aah yee ha, aah yee ha
Which way should I go?
Which way should I go?

While they sang, they danced. They danced in a straight line: *Aah yee ha, aah yee ha*. Then they stopped. *Waa yee seekee ahh kuu, waa yee seekee ahh kuu*. They looked to one side and then to the other: *Which way should I go? Which way should I go?*

Sometimes Joey turned to the left. Sometimes he turned to the right. Sometimes Grandma chose which way to turn and led him all the way through the house.

Sometimes they sang other songs and danced other dances. Sometimes Grandma's feet moved so quickly Joey had trouble keeping up. But *Aah yee ha, aah yee ha* was Joey's favourite song. It sang in his head whenever Grandma asked, "Would you like to play inside or outside?" It danced in his feet when she asked, "Would you like to go to the park or to the beach?"

When Joey was practising adding and subtracting, he sang the song under his breath—*aah yee ha, aah yee ha*—and asked himself: Should I go out and play or should I do my homework? Joey really wanted to play. But it took a lot of work to get ready for a math test, and he liked how it felt when he got the answers correct.

It was the same with soccer practice. When it was cold and rainy, it was hard to leave the cozy couch. Joey really wanted to stay inside and watch TV. But watching TV wouldn't make him a better soccer player. So he put on his soccer boots—*aah yee ha, aah yee ha*—and danced out the door—*waa yee seekee ahh kuu*.

One day Grandma got sick
and died. For many days Joey lay on his bed
with his face in his pillow. Finally he got up and
went outside. But nothing was the same as it had
been before. Joey's best friend, Simon, tried to make Joey
smile. He told Joey funny jokes and made silly faces.

But Joey didn't smile. He told Simon, "Grandma died
and I am not happy."

aBb Cc Dd Ee Ff

At school, Mrs. Walker allowed Joey to skip a math test and a spelling test. She tried to encourage Joey by giving him extra help with his school work. But Joey didn't even want to pick up his pencil.

"Grandma died," he told Mrs. Walker. "I don't want to do my school work."

At the store, Mr. Smith gave Joey a pack of gum and then passed him a bag of groceries. But Joey's arms hurt and he couldn't carry the bag.

"Grandma died," he told Mr. Smith, "and I don't feel very well."

Mom tried to make Joey feel better, too. She made applesauce with cinnamon. She served applesauce with ice cream. She even put raisins in the applesauce. But Joey wasn't hungry.

"No thanks, Mom," he said. "Grandma died and I don't feel like eating."

One day Joey walked past Grandma's house and thought he heard her singing.

Waa yee seekee ahh kuu
Waa yee seekee ahh kuu

Joey said quietly, to no one in particular, "There wasn't any this way or that way this time. I didn't get to choose.

Grandma just died. And she was my
favourite person in the whole world."

The next day when Joey walked past Grandma's house he heard her voice singing again.

Aah yee ha, aah yee ha
Waa yee seekee ahh kuu
Waa yee seekee ahh kuu

Aah yee ha, aah yee ha
Which way should I go?
Which way should I go?

"Stop it!" he said loudly. "I don't want to hear that song ever again."

The following day when Joey heard Grandma's voice and the words to her song he stopped and hollered as loud as he could, "I don't know! I don't know! I don't have a choice. Grandma's gone and she can't come back!"

Joey threw himself onto the grass. He cried, but the song didn't stop. He sobbed and sobbed—but he could still hear the song.

Joey stopped crying and just sniffled for a while. Then he began to think.

Aah yee ha, aah yee ha. "I didn't choose to have Grandma die," he said slowly. "But I can choose to stop crying."

Joey rolled onto his back and stared up at the sunny sky. Then he thought some more.

Waa yee seekee ahh kuu. "That's right," he said, a little steadier than before. "Grandma is gone. I can't choose to bring her back. But I can choose to have a sad face or a happy face."

Joey sat up and looked at Grandma's house. He thought he saw her in the front window, dancing in a circle.

Which way should I go? "I know now," he said determinedly. "Grandma gave me her song. Now I must choose whether or not I will listen to it."

Joey stood up and began to dance.

Aah yee ha, aah yee ha
Waa yee seekee ahh kuu
Waa yee seekee ahh kuu

Aah yee ha, aah yee ha
Which way should I go?
Which way should I go?

Joey sang and danced for a long time.

MILK

When Simon, Mrs. Walker, and Mr. Smith saw Joey again they asked him, “Joey, why do you look so happy?”

Joey told them, “Because I have decided to sing Grandma’s song and dance Grandma’s dance.”

“Will you teach it to us?” they asked.

“One day,” said Joey. “When I am ready.”

Afterword

Ron Martin is the eighth child of Robert Martin Sr. and Cecelia Martin (née Lucas) of Opitsaht. Opitsaht has been the ancestral home of the Martin family for many generations. It is situated on Meares Island, across from Tofino on the west coast of Vancouver Island, British Columbia. Ron's father, Robert, was a hereditary chief (Ha'withl) of the Tla-o-qui-aht (formerly known as Clayoquot), one of the Nuu-chah-nulth First Nations.

One of the main roles of a Ha'withl is to serve the people, and this is what Robert taught his sons. The older sons were taught to fish, hunt, and trap. The younger ones had to stay home because the boat wasn't big enough for all of them.

Ron Martin, the second youngest son, was one who had to stay home, but he was motivated to learn. Robert encouraged his son, telling him, "I'm going to tell you this story. I know you will remember, because you have been given a good memory." Ron was inspired by his father. He worked hard to remember the details of his father's teachings and family history.

Ron now lives and works in Hesquiaht, the ancestral home of his mother, as a First Nations administrator and traditional historian. He actively passes on teachings and Tla-o-qui-aht history to younger generations, including his daughter, Courtney—from whom he can trace back twenty-six generations. In keeping the history alive, he has earned the respect and honour of his family and his community.

The song that is related in this story came from Ron's grandparents, Nan Nuukmiis and Nan Wii-nuk-iinookx. When Ron was young, he and his brothers and sisters often visited their grandparents. Their Nans would take the drum off the wall and start singing songs for the grandchildren. This particular song, "Waa-yee-seekee aakx kuu," is one that all in Ron's family fondly remember. Ron recalls, "When Nan Nuukmiis and Nan Wii-nuk would sing this song, we all danced along and paused, and then we asked ourselves, 'Which way should I go, which way should I go? (*Waa-yee-seekee aakx kuu.*)'"

As Ron explains, this song reminds us that the way we react to everything in life is a choice. In every waking moment of our lives, we should be aware that we have chosen whatever we are doing or thinking. That is why we sing and dance and then pause, to ask ourselves, "Which way should I go?" We can stay in bed or we can get up. We can listen or not listen. We can be angry or not angry. Everything is a choice.

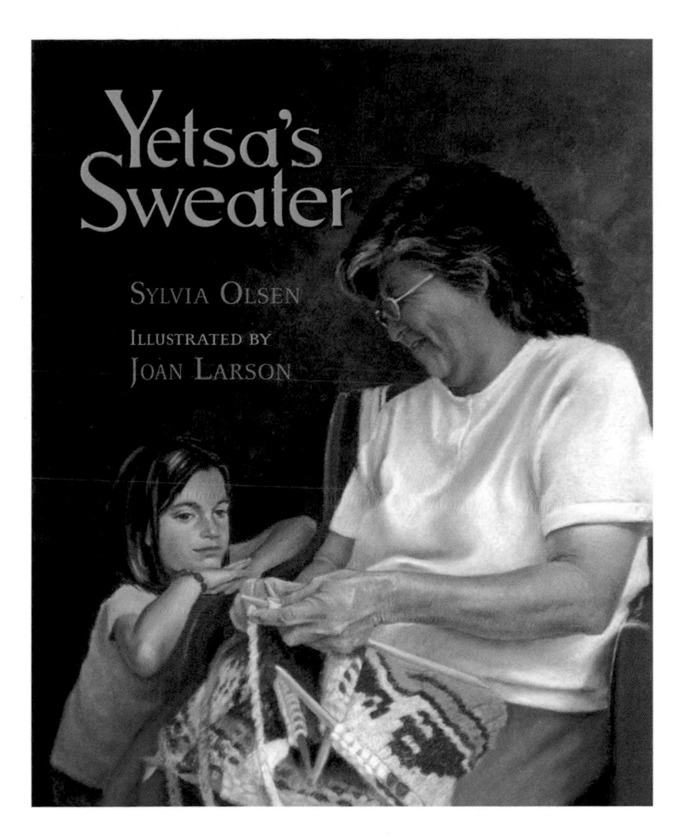

Yetsa's Sweater

Sylvia Olsen   Illustrated by Joan Larson

"What are you knitting into this sweater, Grandma?" Yetsa asks. Grandma smiles. "Flowers. Fish and waves. Woolly clouds, and blackberries."

From the author of *No Time To Say Goodbye*, *Girl with a Baby* and *White Girl* comes a tender and joyful picture book, perfect for sharing. In *Yetsa's Sweater*, Sylvia Olsen takes a workaday chore and illuminates it with meaning, while Joan Larson takes Olsen's simple and loving words and fills them with radiant light.

On a fresh spring day, young Yetsa, her mother and her grandmother gather to prepare the sheep fleeces piled in Grandma's yard. As they clean, wash and dry the fleece, laughter and hard work connect the three generations. Through Yetsa's sensual experience of each task, the reader joins this family in an old but vibrant tradition: the creation of Cowichan sweaters. Each sweater is unique, and its design tells a story. In *Yetsa's Sweater*, that story is one of love, welcome and pride in a job well done.

☆ *Shining Willow Award (Nominee)*

☆ *BC Booksellers' Choice Award (Nominee)*

☆ *Chocolate Lily Award (Nominee)*